HILLERS

Artesian Press

GHOST IN THE DESERT

SUSANNAH BRIN

P.O. Box 355 Buena Park, CA 90621

Take Ten Books
Chillers

Alien Encounter	1-58659-051-
Cassette	1-58659-056-
Ghost in the Desert	**1-58659-052-**
Cassette	**1-58659-057-**
The Haunted Beach House	1-58659-053-
Cassette	1-58659-058-
Trapped in the Sixties	1-58659-054-
Cassette	1-58659-059-
The Water Witch	1-58659-055-
Cassette	1-58659-060-

Other Take Ten Themes:

Mystery
Sports
Adventure
Disaster
Thrillers
Fantasy

Development and Production:Laurel Associates, Inc.
Cover Illustrator:Black Eagle Productions
Cover Designer: Tony Amaro

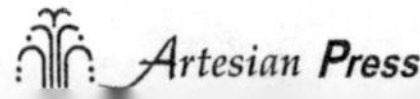

ISBN 1-58659-052

Contents

Chapter 1

The sun was just coming up when Carter Jackson pushed his motocross bike out the garage door. He looked up at the sky and watched as the curtain of darkness slowly gave way to morning.

Glancing at the thermometer, he saw that the temperature had already risen to seventy degrees. In another hour it would be in the eighties. By afternoon, the temperature would be somewhere in the hundreds. *Another summer day in the California desert,* he thought as he swung his leg over his bike.

The street was quiet. People were sleeping. Carter pushed his bike down the driveway to the street. He didn't start the engine because he didn't want to wake up the neighbors. He figured he could push it all the way to the guard gate that stood watch over the resort's gated community. He was just about to move up the street when he heard his mother calling him. Carter stopped and sighed heavily.

"Carter! Carter!" his mother said in a loud whisper. She hurried toward him, clutching her robe around her slender body.

He turned in her direction and waited. His heart sank when he saw the irritated yet determined expression on her face. Her brown eyes, the same color as his, seemed almost black in the morning light. There would be no getting away now. He stared at her short blond hair. Rumpled from sleep, it stuck straight out from her head like wires. Somehow it reminded him of her prizewinning terrier, Murphy.

"Just where do you think you're going, Carter?" She stared up at him, not the least bit intimidated by his height of six feet, two inches.

"Why, I'm going out to ride in the desert—just like I do every morning, Mom. I have a big bike race coming up, remember?"

"Well, you'll just have to wait until Denise Baker goes home. She'll only be here for a couple of weeks."

Carter stared at his mother in disbelief. "A couple of *weeks*? But the race is just four weeks away!"

"Sorry, but it can't be helped. I told you yesterday that you would have to entertain her while she's here. She's the daughter of my best friend from college. I promised her mother we'd show her a good time."

"Why don't *you* show her a good time then," snapped Carter. "I didn't ask her to come here."

"I can't. This week I have to take Murphy to the Palm Springs Dog Show. I've already paid the entrance fees. I want *you* to entertain her, Carter. It's only for a week. She's a lovely girl." His mother smiled brightly at him.

Denise Baker is more than lovely, thought Carter. *She's beautiful.* After he'd met her the night before, he couldn't stop sneaking glances at her. She was a tall girl with long, reddish hair. "I don't know, Mom. I'm not very good at socializing," argued Carter, avoiding his mother's eyes.

"Nonsense! You can be perfectly charming when you want to be. Now come back into the house and have breakfast," commanded his mother.

Hearing her no-nonsense tone, he knew he had no choice unless he wanted to start World War III. "All right—but one week only. I've got my race to worry about," grumbled Carter.

When he entered the kitchen, his father and Denise were already sitting at the table, drinking juice. As Carter crossed the large room, his mother's terrier, Murphy, dashed across the floor and attached his sharp little teeth to the cuff of Carter's jeans.

Carter shook Murphy off, making the dog jump back and growl.

His mother laughed and picked up the tiny dog. "Murphy, don't bite Carter. He loves you," she scolded.

"Right," mumbled Carter, taking a carton of milk from the fridge.

Mr. Jackson lowered his newspaper and turned to Denise. "As you can see, Murphy is rather high-strung. That's what I hate about purebreds. Give me a mutt anytime. Now *those* dogs know how to behave."

Mrs. Jackson gave her husband a frown. "Oh, Murphy's just having fun. He likes to play tug of war." Cooing to her dog, she left the kitchen.

"*Playing?* That dog would like to kill us all," Carter grumbled as he pulled out a chair and sat down.

"I think you may be right, my boy.

Luckily, all of us are a lot bigger than Murphy," laughed his father.

Glancing sideways, Carter saw Denise smiling. Pleased that he had gotten her to smile, he continued. "Dad, that dog is a little beast. I've got scars to prove it."

Carrying his coffee cup to the sink, Mr. Jackson nodded. "I'm sure you do. But the scars probably came from that darn cycle you're always riding. Well, I must be off to work now. Have a good day, you two."

In a moment, Carter could hear his father's car start and then back down the driveway. Upstairs, he could hear his mother calling Murphy. It was quiet in the kitchen. His heart raced. He didn't know what to say to Denise.

"Do you *really* have scars from Murphy?" asked Denise, trying to make conversation.

Swallowing a mouthful of cereal, Carter shook his head. "No, I was just exaggerating. But I do have some pants that arc shredded at the cuff."

Denise giggled, then stopped. "I'm sorry. I don't mean to laugh. It's just that the way he growls and flies across the floor to attack seems so funny."

Carter laughed, too. "Yeah. He thinks he's a doberman."

"Some of my friends have tiny dogs. Sometimes I just want to punt those little yappy dogs across the room. Of course, I would never do such a thing. But I must admit that the thought has crossed my mind," Denise confided in a low voice.

Surprised that she felt the same way he did, Carter felt himself loosening up. "I know what you mean," he grinned, and then added, "Murphy is okay—when he's asleep."

Denise laughed again. Then she became serious. "I'm sorry that I got dumped on you. My parents are having some marriage problems. I guess they thought if they could get away together for a while, they might be able to sort everything out."

"That's too bad," said Carter. He saw the hurt in her eyes, and his heart went out to her. He couldn't imagine his own parents fighting. "Look, you want to ride out in the desert with me? I need to practice for a race. You could sit in the shade and read."

"Sure. I'd like that," answered Denise, glad that he wanted her to go.

"You might want to wear boots and long pants," suggested Carter. Suddenly in a good mood, he stood and carried his cereal bowl to the sink.

"Won't I be too warm?" She had never been in the desert, but she knew it could get really hot.

"Yeah. But boots and long pants are safer to wear than shorts. There are rattlesnakes where we're going," he said matter-of-factly.

Chapter 2

Denise held onto Carter's waist as they rode through the small town of Desert Hot Springs. Heat waves rose from the pavement. Hot wind blew into their faces. Under her helmet, Denise could feel the sweat forming on her scalp. She looked at the back of Carter's neck. It was tanned a deep golden-brown. She smiled to herself, glad that he had invited her to ride along.

Carter slowed the bike as he left the main road and headed into the open desert. He turned his head sideways. "Are you okay back there?" he yelled.

"I'm fine," Denise yelled back.

"Well, hold on! I'm going to crank up the speed." He felt Denise tighten her hold on his waist as he shifted and gave the cycle some gas. Speeding across the wide, sandy floor of the desert, Carter drove around some bleached-white boulders and spiny cactuses. Brown rabbits, roadrunners, and ground squirrels scurried out of the bike's path. Nearing a patch of pepper trees, Carter stopped.

Denise headed for the shade of the trees. "An oasis! I can't believe it!" she cried as she spotted a riverbed. "Oh, darn, there's no water."

"In the winter when we get rain, this dry bed becomes a raging river," Carter explained. "In the summer the water dries up."

"I wish there was some here now," said Denise, disappointed. She took off her helmet and shook out her long hair. "Whew! It sure is hot out here."

"Yeah, but not nearly as hot as it will get as the day goes on." He frowned, worried now that he shouldn't have brought her along. He was used to the high temperatures. She wasn't. Her white skin was already blotchy with spots of red, and the hair curling around her face was damp. "Is the heat too much for you?"

"No, I'm fine. Really. Please don't worry about me," she said, giving him a big smile.

Carter slid off the backpack he'd been wearing and dropped it next to the tree. Then he quickly unzipped it and pulled out an old baseball hat. "Here. This will help shade your face."

"Thanks." Denise twisted her long hair into a knot on top of her head, then pulled on the cap to keep it in place.

"There's a bottle of water in the pack if you get thirsty," Carter said.

Carter kept glancing out at the desert and then back to her. Denise could tell that he was itching to get back on his bike. "Look, I'll be fine. Go on." She gave him another big smile.

Carter grinned. "Okay. I'm just

going to ride over to those hills and do a few climbs and jumps."

Denise watched him as he rode off. Within minutes, he was a dark speck against the bone-white background of the desert. Like smoke signals, puffs of dust showed where he was. Denise wasn't afraid of being left alone. She'd grown up in Seattle, Washington, and was familiar with the outdoors.

After resting in the shade and drinking some water, she decided to walk along the riverbed toward the mountains.

As Denise began to walk, she saw the desert come alive. Everywhere she looked, she noticed something she hadn't seen before. Tiny red ants swarmed on mounds of sand. Road-runners streaked ahead of her, their long tails lifting and lowering like wing flaps on an airplane. Hummingbirds flitted from bush to bush. The rocks she picked up sparkled brightly with flecks of mica and little chunks of fool's gold.

Fascinated by the richness of the desert, she lost track of time as she walked on. Overhead, the sun blazed. The air shimmered with heat. Reaching a group of huge rocks, Denise sat and rested. She wiped her sweat-drenched face with the back of her arm. Wishing she had brought the water bottle, she looked back toward her starting place. In the distance, she could just make out the pepper trees.

I should head back, she thought, but she didn't have the energy to move. A clucking sound startled her. A mother quail and her babies scurried by, moving from cactus to dried bush to rocks. Denise laughed with relief. Then she noticed a small house a few yards farther on. *Funny, I didn't see that before,* she thought. *Must be because I'd kept my head down, looking for rattlesnakes.* Curious, she forgot the heat and started walking toward the lonely little house.

As she neared the place, Denise called out, "Anybody home?" Getting no answer, she walked closer and saw that the house was deserted. The front door was hanging off its hinges, and the windows were broken. Rusted cans and old lumber lay abandoned in the yard. Denise glanced inside but didn't go in. For some odd reason, the place gave her the creeps. She glanced at her watch and saw that it was one o'clock.

I'd better go back, she thought. *Carter is probably looking for me.* But then, out of the corner of her eye, she saw something move. Just ahead, shimmering in the heat like a mirage, was a beautiful young woman with long blond hair!

Denise stared as the young woman seemed to rise in the air. She floated upwards before disappearing into the long shadow created by the mountain.

Denise felt lightheaded. Suddenly she couldn't breathe the hot, thick air. The last thing she remembered was a spinning sensation. Then she was falling, falling into darkness.

When Carter returned to the pepper trees where Denise had been resting, he saw that she was gone. Worried, he scanned the desert, but he didn't see her. Jumping on his bike, he rode toward the mountains, hoping she had followed the dry streambed. Guilt swept over him in waves. "What a fool I was to leave her alone for so long," he muttered to himself.

As he sped toward the mountains, he prayed she was all right. So many bad things could happen to a person in the desert—snakebite, sunstroke, a dangerous encounter with a coyote.

Then, nearing the old house, Carter saw Denise lying on the ground. Fear gripped his chest.

Chapter 3

It was late afternoon. The sun was falling in the west, crowning the surrounding mountains with a blaze of reds and oranges. The temperature was in the low nineties, offering some relief from the afternoon's high of 109 degrees.

Carter sat on the patio, staring at the ice melting in his lemonade. His mother was lecturing him about the dangers of the desert. He knew the dangers, but he didn't say anything. It was his fault that Denise was resting upstairs with possible sunstroke. He felt bad, really bad, about leaving her. *I'm a selfish idiot,* he thought to himself.

"Carter? Are you listening to me?" asked Mrs. Jackson sharply.

He nodded and looked out at the swimming pool, where Murphy was barking at his reflection.

Mrs. Jackson frowned before going on. "As I was saying, it was totally irresponsible of you to leave Denise to fend for herself while you went off riding your bike. *Really,* Carter, you're seventeen years old. I'm surprised you didn't know better."

"I'm sorry. I thought she'd stay in the shade of those big pepper trees," Carter explained wearily.

"That's my point. You didn't *think!*" exclaimed Mrs. Jackson, her dark eyes snapping with irritation. "The poor girl was probably bored out of her mind."

"I wasn't bored at all," Denise objected. Looking refreshed, she stepped out onto the patio. Carter saw that she had showered and changed into a white summer dress.

"Oh, my dear! You should be upstairs resting," Mrs. Jackson said with concern.

"No, really. I'm fine," said Denise. She glanced at Carter and smiled.

She really does look fine, Carter thought to himself. He liked the way she had pulled her red hair up into a pile of curls on top of her head.

"Don't you think you should stay indoors with the air conditioning, my dear? It's still quite warm out here," fussed Mrs. Jackson.

"No, I like the heat. Maybe not as hot as it got today—but it's comfortable now," laughed Denise.

Mrs. Jackson walked to the edge of the shaded patio and called to Murphy. She turned back toward Denise and said, "I'm sorry you had such a horrible first day." She called to Murphy again. Again, the little dog ignored her.

"It wasn't horrible at all. I loved being in the desert. I never realized that there were so many living things out there. All those interesting plants and birds," Denise said with a smile.

"It was foolish of Carter to take you out there in the heat of the day," argued Mrs. Jackson. Bending down, she tried to grab Murphy, but he growled playfully and jumped away.

"No, it was foolish of *me.* I should have stayed in the shade. I didn't mean to walk so far, but then I saw that old house and . . ." Catching a warning look from Carter, Denise stopped and pretended to be interested in Murphy. She called to him and scooped him up.

"Why, thank you, dear," said Mrs. Jackson, taking the tiny terrier from her. She held the dog up to her face. "Shall we take Carter and Denise to the show with us tonight, Murphy? So they can see you win Best of Breed?"

Carter groaned, but then he got an idea. He opened the sliding door for his mother. "I was thinking of taking Denise out to dinner at the Coyote Cafe. Then, when it gets cooler, I thought we could walk down the strip in Palm Springs. Look in the stores."

Mrs. Jackson raised an eyebrow at her son. She knew he was trying to get out of going to the dog show. He hated dog shows as much as he hated shopping. But she finally agreed, thinking Denise would enjoy herself.

Much later, seated at a table in the Coyote Cafe, Carter apologized to Denise. "I'm really sorry about today. I guess I just lost track of time."

"It's not your fault. *I* wanted to go with you, remember?" Denise insisted. "Besides, I should have taken some water with me." Grinning, she reached for her glass of lemonade. She still felt kind of dehydrated.

"It never occurred to me you would go for a walk, Denise. And such a *long* walk. I was really scared when I got back to the trees and you were gone. Then, when I found you lying on the ground, I was terrified," admitted Carter, unable to keep his eyes on hers.

"How did you know where to look?" asked Denise. She took a bite of her taco salad.

Carter shrugged. "Just a hunch. I asked myself where *I* would go walking if I didn't want to get lost."

"I knew that if I stayed by the riverbed, I could find my way back. Oh, how come you didn't want me saying anything about the deserted house to your mom?"

Carter frowned, wondering how much to tell her. For the past year, he'd been drawn to that same house. The first time he'd come upon it was purely by accident. But he hadn't forgotten what he'd seen there. The thought of it still chilled him to the bone.

Denise could tell by the intense expression on Carter's face that he was wrestling with the idea of whether to tell her or not. She leaned toward him. "Tell me, Carter, *please.*"

Carter hunched his shoulders and

leaned forward, his eyes on his empty plate. "Ten years ago, there was a murder at that house."

"Really? A *murder?*" Denise felt her heart race as she waited for him to continue.

"I was only seven, but everybody was talking about it. It was on TV and in the papers. A young woman was shot to death. Her husband was in Los Angeles on business. The police never found the murderer."

"What did she look like?"

So *she* had seen something, too! Seeing the intense interest in Denise's face, Carter felt a loosening in his chest. Maybe he wasn't crazy after all. But he had to be sure they were on the same wavelength. "I don't know. Why? Did *you* see something?" he asked, watching her carefully.

Denise blushed. She felt foolish. She didn't want to tell him she'd seen a ghost. But Carter pressed her to answer.

Finally, she whispered, "I saw a pretty young woman with long blond hair. She was walking along the riverbed toward the mountains." Suddenly feeling uncomfortable and a bit silly, she tried to shrug it off. "It was probably just a mirage."

Carter felt like he was going to explode with excitement. *"I've seen her, too!"* he cried. Realizing that people were looking in his direction, he lowered his voice. "I think she's a ghost. A spirit. I've never told anyone. I was afraid they would think I was out of my mind. Like you, I convinced myself that it must have been the heat. But now you've seen her, too."

Denise frowned. "But *why* is she there?"

"I don't know," Carter said. "But we're going to find out."

Chapter 4

It was another hot day in the desert, but Carter and Denise didn't feel the heat. They were in the air-conditioned Palm Springs public library, studying books and microfilm. It was Carter's idea to do a little research before they ventured out to the old house again. Denise agreed. She was curious about the young woman. Very curious. But she wasn't in any big hurry to see the beautiful ghost again.

Denise was sitting at a table, leafing through books about ghosts and spirits, when Carter walked up to her with several photocopied pages. She could see by his expression that he had found what he was looking for. Marking her place in her book, she turned to him.

"I found several newspaper articles about the murder," Carter explained in a hushed voice. "It took me a while because the old newspapers are all on microfilm." He handed Denise the copies he'd made of the articles.

Denise shivered and felt herself grow even colder as she read the article, dated August 12, 1987:

MURDER IN THE DESERT

The body of Daisy Robbins was found next to a dry riverbed in the desert just north of the city of Desert Hot Springs. She had been shot twice in the back sometime around noon or one o'clock. According to detectives, the twenty-five-year-old wife of David Robbins had been running from her killer at the time of her death. David Robbins has been eliminated as a suspect since he was in Los Angeles on business at the time. The police do not have any suspects. Anyone with information is asked to contact the local police.

Denise studied the picture of Daisy Robbins that accompanied the article. She looked at Carter with astonishment. "Daisy Robbins is the same woman I saw yesterday by the riverbank."

Carter nodded. "I know. When I saw this photograph, I couldn't believe it either. What I can't figure out is why she appeared to us."

Now it was Denise's turn to be excited. "I don't think she picked us."

"Huh?"

Seeing the confusion on Carter's face, Denise said, "I think anyone who goes out there around the time she was killed can see her. Read this." Denise picked up the book she'd been reading and handed it to Carter.

When Carter finished reading, he looked at Denise and smiled. "The writer says that a spirit stays on earth because it is not at rest—maybe even in pain. That makes sense. Being shot would sure be painful."

Denise rolled her eyes. "Get serious, Carter. The reason Daisy Robbins' spirit can't find peace is because her murder hasn't been solved."

"So you think her spirit will stay out there in the desert until someone finds the murderer?" asked Carter, beginning to understand.

"That's what this book says. All of these other books, too," said Denise, pointing to the pile of books on the table in front of her. "I think we have to find her murderer."

Carter frowned and shook his head. He wondered if Denise's time in the desert had affected her. She was talking as though she had lost a few brain cells. "It's been ten years since the murder, Denise. *Ten years.* It's what the police call an unsolved mystery."

"I know, but . . ." she hesitated for a moment. "Yesterday, when I saw the young woman, it seemed to me that she wanted me to follow her."

Thinking back to the times he'd seen the spirit, Carter remembered the young woman walking north along the riverbed. But he hadn't felt her wanting him to follow. "I didn't feel that."

Denise shrugged. "Maybe she only speaks to other women."

"Makes sense. Girls are always sharing secrets with each other," teased Carter, grinning.

Annoyed, Denise pushed back her chair and stood up. She glared at Carter. "Well, aren't you the least bit curious about where she was going?"

"Of course I am." Carter jumped up. He could see the fire in Denise's green eyes. He didn't want her to be angry. "Look, I was just teasing, okay?"

"Okay." Denise didn't know why she was feeling so uptight. *It's probably this whole ghost thing,* she told herself. It was spooky; scary.

Carter glanced at the large clock on the wall. It was twenty past noon.

If Denise's theory was correct, they still had forty minutes to get out to the deserted house before the ghost disappeared. He stuffed the copies into his back pocket. "Let's go. I figure if we hurry, we can still catch Daisy's spirit walking by the riverbed."

"Great," said Denise, excitement flushing her face.

Outside, hot air rushed into their chests, making it hard to breathe.

Carter revved the bike's engine as Denise tightened her grip around his waist. Then he turned sideways and looked at her. "You *sure* you want to go out there in this heat?"

"Is it going to be cooler tomorrow?" she asked, knowing the answer.

"No. Could be hotter. I just don't want you to get sick, like yesterday." Concern filled Carter's face.

"I didn't get sick. I fainted. I just wasn't used to the heat. I'm okay. Let's go," urged Denise, giving him a big smile to show that she'd be fine.

"Okay." He stepped on the gas, and the bike leapt forward in a burst of speed. "We're off to see the spirit!" yelled Carter as he steered the bike out of the parking lot and onto the main highway.

"I think the song goes, 'We're off to see the wizard'!" laughed Denise.

"I knew that," Carter yelled back. He'd been trying to make a joke. Inside, he felt anxious. A ghost woman was waiting for them in the desert. Was it the spirit of Daisy Robbins?

Chapter 5

Hot, dry wind was blowing as they came to the deserted house. Carter parked the bike and climbed off. Denise took off her helmet and shook out her hair. It was already damp. "It's a furnace out here today," she mumbled as she wiped her forehead with the back of her arm.

Carter glanced at her anxiously. "Are you okay?"

"Sure!" Denise glanced toward the dry riverbed. She shivered in the heat as fear gripped her. In the distance, she could see the spirit of Daisy Robbins walking among the rocks. "There she is. Do you see her?"

"Do I ever!" answered Carter, his stomach suddenly doing flipflops. He glanced at Denise. "There's no doubting she's a real spirit now. Not if we both see her at the same time."

"No doubt at all," murmured Denise. The sight of the dead woman made her feel very shaken and lightheaded. Taking a deep breath, she forced herself to stay calm.

Sensing their presence, the spirit turned and stared in their direction. "She's watching us," whispered Carter, feeling more anxious by the minute.

"I know. She's so beautiful and young. She looks so sad," said Denise. Tears sprang to her eyes. Quickly, she wiped them away. "I think she's waiting for us to follow her."

Carter nodded. He was reluctant to start moving. Then, sensing that Denise was waiting for him, he straightened his shoulders. "Right. But I don't think we should get too close," he warned.

Denise walked by Carter's side. Careful to keep a safe distance from the spirit, they followed Daisy Robbins up the riverbed. Occasionally, the spirit would look back over her shoulder, as if to reassure herself that Denise and Carter were still there.

Heat rose from the desert floor in shimmering waves. The sun seemed to burn through their clothes. Yet neither of them seemed to notice the heat. It was as though the spirit woman had hypnotized them.

Reaching a sharp bend in the dry riverbed, Daisy Robbins stopped. Carter and Denise stopped, too. They watched as Daisy bent down and began turning over rocks.

"What is she doing now?" asked Carter, wiping the sweat from his face.

"Seems to me that she's looking for something," whispered Denise, straining to see. She wished they could walk closer to the spirit woman, but she didn't want to frighten her away.

As Carter and Denise watched, the

spirit tried to move a large rock. But it was too heavy for her. Again and again she tried. Finally she gave up and stood facing them. Her shoulders shook with silent tears.

"What should we do?" asked Denise, upset at seeing the spirit sobbing.

"I don't know. Wait, I guess," whispered Carter. He thought it was odd that they could see the spirit crying, but could hear no sound.

After several minutes, the spirit of Daisy Robbins lifted her head and stared straight at Denise and Carter. Denise grabbed Carter's arm. She wanted to run away—and yet she didn't. She felt sorry for Daisy Robbins. Finally, she got up the courage to ask, "What do you want us to do?"

Daisy Robbins stared sadly at Denise. Then she turned and looked down at the rocks in the riverbed.

"What?" asked Carter. He felt bad

for the beautiful spirit woman, too.

The spirit of Daisy Robbins looked at them again. Then she just seemed to disappear into the sunlight—like water drying up.

"Look! She's gone!" cried Denise, stumbling forward. She looked back at Carter. "What does she want us to do?"

"Come on. Let's go check out those large rocks she was trying to move," suggested Carter. He was feeling edgy, too. Together they started turning over rocks in the riverbed. It was hard work. The broiling midday sun quickly sapped their energy.

Denise stood up first. She put her hands on her lower back and stretched. She was breathing heavily. "Maybe we should try moving these larger rocks." She pointed to several grayish-white boulders.

"Okay," said Carter. "If we both get on one side, I think we can roll them." Starting with the largest boulder, they pushed. The rock moved slowly forward. "One more push and I think we've got it," said Carter.

The boulder inched forward, then finally rolled and tumbled away. They searched the ground where it had been. Nothing. Nothing but sand.

Denise pointed to another boulder. Again, they rolled the rock away. But again, nothing was underneath. Denise needed a drink of water. Her mouth felt as dry as the desert floor. "I wish we had brought some bottled water."

Carter glanced at her with concern. "We should stop now and come back tomorrow. The worst thing that can happen to you in the desert is to become dehydrated."

"I know. Your mother told me," said Denise. She could feel her skin burning. "Let's just move this last big rock. If we don't find anything, we'll come back tomorrow."

The last boulder was fairly easy to

move. It rolled forward and crashed down into the riverbed. "Look!" yelled Carter, pointing at a pile of small rocks under the larger rock.

Denise knelt and began throwing the rocks to the side. When she had cleared all the rocks, she looked up at Carter and shook her head. "There's nothing here. Just sand."

"In the winter, water rushes down from the mountains, carrying rocks and boulders and sand," explained Carter. "Maybe there's something buried here." Quickly, he dug down into the sand and dirt. He was about to give up when his fingers hit something hard. Digging a little deeper, he saw it.

"Oh, *my!*" cried Denise. "It's a gun."

Carter carefully lifted the old gun from its hiding place. He shook away the sand and inspected it. "I don't know much about guns, but this one looks like some kind of revolver."

"It's the gun that murdered Daisy

Robbins. I just *know* it!" cried Denise, excitedly. "This is what she wanted us to find."

"I think so, too," Carter said. "So what do we do now?"

"We take the gun to the police." Denise turned and started walking back toward the old house where they'd parked the motorcycle.

Carter hurried to catch up. "I don't know if they can do much with this old gun. It's rusted. If it *is* the murder weapon, it's been out here for ten years. Any fingerprints would be long gone."

"The police have lots of new ways to test guns, Carter. Maybe they can find out who owned it. Let's go straight to the police station."

Nodding, Carter started his bike as Denise climbed on.

Chapter 6

Before going to the police station, Carter and Denise stopped at a small grocery store. Denise bought two bottles of water. When she returned to the bike, she handed Carter one of the bottles and a brown paper bag.

"I think you should put the gun in the bag," suggested Denise. She took a long drink of her water. She couldn't remember a time when she'd ever been so thirsty.

Carter finished drinking his water, then looked at Denise with questioning eyes. "Put the gun in the bag?"

Denise gave him an exasperated look. "We can't just go walking into the police station waving a gun. They might shoot us."

"I think you've seen too many cop shows," teased Carter. But he did as she said, thinking she might have a point. Then they were off to the station.

The air conditioning in the police station felt good to both of them. Before heading for the main desk, Carter stopped and turned to Denise. He pulled the pages he'd copied at the library from his pocket. His eyes skimmed the article. "It says here that a Tom Anderson was the detective on the case. That's who we should ask to see," Carter whispered.

They walked up to the front desk. "We'd like to see Detective Tom Anderson," Carter said to the police officer standing there.

"What about?" asked the officer.

"We have something for him," said Denise, looking straight at the man with a determined expression.

"Oh, I see. A little secret," joked the officer. He lifted the phone and called

Tom Anderson. "I've got a couple of young people here to see you, Tom. Shall I send them back?" He listened and then hung up the phone. "This way. I'll take you to his office."

Denise glanced at Carter. She'd never been in a police station before. It all seemed a little scary. Carter threw her a wink of reassurance as they followed the young cop to the small offices in back. He left them at a glass door marked *Detective Tom Anderson.*

A large, darkly tanned man waved them in without getting up from his chair. "Take a seat and tell me what I can do for you."

They sat, and Carter immediately started talking. He introduced himself and Denise. "Sir, we read in the papers that you were the detective on the Robbins murder." Carter felt nervous. He'd never talked to a detective before.

Tom Anderson leaned forward and stared hard at Carter, then Denise.

"That's right. Ten years and we still haven't found the killer. I doubt that we ever will."

"Is the case still open?" asked Denise.

Tom Anderson smiled. "There's no statute of limitations on murder. That is, we never close a murder case. We've got some on the books that are more than fifty years old."

"Wow," said Carter, starting to feel more at ease. "I bet the murderer is dead by now."

"Some might be. Depends on how young the killer was at the time," the detective answered. He frowned at Carter, hoping to discourage further questions. He didn't have all day to sit around chatting with teenagers. "So let's hear it. What's this big secret you wanted to tell me?"

Carter glanced at Denise, and she nodded for him to go ahead. "Well, sir, we were out in the desert by the Robbins house and we found this," explained Carter. He handed the brown paper bag to the detective.

Tom Anderson took the gun out of the bag and stared at it.

"We were thinking it might be the murder weapon. You know, the gun that killed Daisy Robbins," added Denise, talking quickly.

"And what made you think that?" asked Tom Anderson, giving them both a questioning look.

Carter stumbled over his words, suddenly nervous again. "We found it a couple hundred yards from the house—in the dry riverbed."

"Uh huh. So what were you two doing out there, besides getting bad sunburns?" The detective eyed them sharply, waiting for more information.

"Nothing, really," Denise said quickly. "I mean we were just riding

Carter's motorcycle. He goes out there to practice for motocross races. I just went along with him for the ride."

Tom Anderson looked at the gun one last time and then put it on his desk. He stood up and smiled at them. "I don't know if this gun is connected to the Robbins murder or not. But I'll look into it. You did the right thing bringing the gun here. Thank you."

Carter and Denise both stood up. They smiled shyly and started to leave. At the door, Carter turned back. "Will you let us know if it was the gun that killed Daisy Robbins?"

"*Please,* Mr. Anderson," added Denise. "We're kind of curious."

Tom Anderson shook his head as if he'd seen and heard it all. "Sure. But don't go getting your hopes up. Finding a gun doesn't always solve a mystery."

Chapter 7

The rest of that week rushed by without a single word from Detective Anderson. There was nothing Carter and Denise could do but wait. Denise had a bad sunburn. Carter tried to find ways to amuse her. They went shopping in Palm Springs, explored the other desert cities, and swam in the pool. But the gun weighed heavily on their minds. They talked about it every day as their curiosity grew.

On Tuesday of the following week, they were sitting on the patio playing cards when the doorbell rang. Murphy, who had won several ribbons in his dog show, raced in circles, barking.

"*Quiet,* Murphy! I wonder who that is," said Carter, putting his cards down and starting for the front door.

"Maybe it's your mother back from her luncheon," said Denise, reaching down to pick up Murphy. The little dog licked her face.

"Denise, it's Detective Anderson," grinned Carter. He led the older man into the living room.

Surprised and delighted, Denise put Murphy down and walked toward the detective. Murphy growled and sped across the room. Before the detective could shoo away the tiny terrier, Murphy had grabbed onto a piece of his pantleg.

"Murphy!" Carter snapped, angrily. He reached down and pulled the dog off the detective's pantleg. "I'm sorry. I'm afraid he isn't the most sociable dog in the world."

"If that mutt was mine, it would learn some manners or lose its teeth," growled Tom Anderson.

Embarrassed, Carter motioned for

the detective to sit in the big, white overstuffed chair. Carter and Denise sat opposite him on a matching sofa. They leaned toward the detective, eager to hear what he'd learned about the gun.

Tom Anderson could tell from the expressions on their faces that the two teenagers were excited. "I wanted to tell you about what's happened since you gave me the gun. It will be in the newspapers tomorrow and on television tonight," said Tom, drawing out the suspense.

"What?" gasped Carter and Denise at the same time.

The detective laughed, and then grew serious. "You two were right. The gun that you found *was* the murder weapon. We did some ballistic tests. The grooving inside the barrel matched the grooving on the bullets that killed Daisy Robbins."

"Wow! After ten years you were still able to tell that?" asked Carter, impressed with the technology. He glanced sideways at Denise. She smiled as if to say, "I told you so."

"Did you find out who owned the gun?" asked Denise, eager to know everything.

"Hold your horses, young lady," chuckled Tom. "I'm getting to that part of the story. I don't know if you know this—but right after the body was found, we thought the husband, David Robbins, had done it. But he had an alibi. Said he was up in Los Angeles on business. His alibi checked out. His secretary Lila Sims was with him, and she backed up his story."

"Maybe she was lying," piped up Denise. She'd seen a lot of cop shows. In most of them, someone always turned out to be lying.

Tom Anderson gave Denise a sharp look and nodded his head. "That's what I thought at the time, too. Something fishy about the way the two of them looked at each other when we questioned them. But you can't put someone in jail just because they act funny. Besides, we didn't have a murder weapon or any eyewitnesses."

"All you had was the dead body of Daisy Robbins," added Carter.

"That's right. And the dead don't talk," said Tom Anderson.

Carter glanced at Denise. He could tell that she was thinking the same thing that he was. Daisy Robbins *had* spoken to them. Not in words—but in showing herself to them, leading them to the weapon.

Tom Anderson caught the glance that passed between the teens. He knew they were holding something back. "As I was saying—the dead don't talk. But sometimes we get lucky. While they were running tests on the gun, I tracked down its owner."

"How did you do that?" asked Carter, fascinated with every detail.

"Serial numbers. All guns are registered with their serial numbers. Guess who owned the gun?" asked Tom Anderson. He seemed to enjoy stretching out his story.

"Who?" asked Carter and Denise. They were almost ready to burst with curiosity.

"The husband. David Robbins." Detective Anderson leaned back in his chair and smiled with satisfaction.

"So he *was* lying!" Denise whooped, excitedly.

"Yep. He even lied about owning a gun. Said he didn't believe in firearms. Too dangerous." Tom Anderson shook his head wearily.

"Anyway, we tracked down David Robbins this week and arrested him for the murder of his wife, Daisy."

"Where was he?" asked Carter, thinking that after ten years the killer might have left the country.

"Up in Los Angeles. Living in a big

mansion with his new wife, Lila Sims," answered Tom Anderson.

"The secretary that had lied for him!" cried Denise. The puzzle pieces were all falling together in her mind.

"Exactly. Seems the young Daisy Robbins had inherited a lot of money. In her will she left everything to her husband, David."

"And he killed her for the money—so he could run off with Lila Sims! How awful. Poor Daisy." Denise's eyes filled with tears as she thought about the beautiful woman, dying so young.

"Unfortunately, we can't undo what happened then. But at least now, Mr. Robbins and Lila Sims will be spending the rest of their lives behind bars where they belong," sighed Tom Anderson, standing up. "Thanks to you two, justice has finally been served. Daisy Robbins can rest in peace."

"I hope so," murmured Carter, wondering if the spirit of Daisy Robbins would now be able to leave the earthly plane. "We'll soon find out," he muttered to himself.

"What did you say?" asked Tom Anderson, not quite hearing what Carter had mumbled.

"Nothing. Just thinking out loud," answered Carter. He considered telling the detective about the spirit, but then decided against it. After all, the detective was a man used to dealing in cold, hard facts.

Tom Anderson had a gut feeling that the two young people weren't telling him everything they knew. But it didn't matter. The case was solved.

After the detective left, Carter and Denise headed straight for the garage where Carter's motorcycle was parked.

Chapter 8

Carter drove his motorcycle at top speed. He wanted to reach the old abandoned house before one o'clock—before the spirit of Daisy Robbins vanished. Denise kept looking at her wristwatch. She was anxious, too.

The sun was hot, as usual. *Another scorching day in the desert,* thought Denise. But she was beginning to get used to the heat. It didn't sap her strength the way it had that first day.

Carter veered off the highway onto the desert floor. He headed toward the Robbins' old house. Nothing moved in the desert, except the cycle. The roar of the bike cut through the quiet like a police siren in the middle of the night.

Again, he parked near the deserted house. Denise dismounted and waited for Carter. Checking her watch, she saw that it was ten minutes to one. She stared in the direction of the riverbed, letting her eyes travel toward the mountains. "There she is," cried Denise, making out the figure of Daisy Robbins in the distance.

"Let's go, Denise! We only have five minutes before she disappears," said Carter.

Together, they took off running. When they were within a hundred yards of the spirit, they stopped. "Do you think we should tell her that her murder has been solved?" asked Carter.

"I don't know," said Denise with a frown. "I don't even know if she can hear us. Remember when we tried asking her what was wrong? She didn't respond."

"It's worth a try," said Carter, wanting to relieve the dead woman's worried mind. He shot Denise a long, questioning look.

Denise smiled to hide the fear beating in her chest. "I think we have to try. After all, that's why we came out here, right?" She could clearly see the dead woman, Daisy Robbins. The spirit looked so young, standing there in a long sundress, her blond hair falling loosely down her back.

Carter coughed, clearing his throat. He felt nervous. After another quick glance at Denise for courage, he yelled, "Daisy! Your murder has been solved! We found the gun and took it to Detective Anderson. He traced it to your husband, David. And he's admitted to killing you. He's in jail." Carter stopped and turned to Denise. "Should I tell her that his new wife, Lila Sims, is also in jail?"

Denise shook her head no. "She probably already knows. It would only make her sadder to remind her."

"Right. Well, then what else can I say?" asked Carter, watching the spirit turn slowly toward them.

"She's looking at us," cried Denise, grabbing hold of Carter's arm.

As they watched, the spirit of Daisy Robbins smiled at them. She raised her hand and waved. Then, in the blink of an eye, she was gone. It was as though she had faded into the shimmering heat waves coming off the desert.

"Wow! Did you see her wave at us?" exclaimed Carter. It was hard to believe what he had just seen. But he knew that it had happened. Denise had seen it, too.

"Yes. And I think she's gone for good this time." Denise smiled. She was glad that the dead woman would no longer be troubled and in pain.

"Maybe now Daisy Robbins can rest in peace," said Carter. He felt a rush of hope fill his body. He grinned crazily at Denise.

Denise was smiling, too. She felt the same rush of hope. Looking around at the desert, she could see that it was blooming with life. A gray digger squirrel popped up from its hole and scooted across to a yucca plant. Hummingbirds chased each other from bush to bush. A roadrunner strutted along the dry riverbed.

As they started back toward Carter's motorcycle, Denise laughed. "What's so funny?" he asked.

"Nothing. I guess I just feel good. You know—glad to be alive." Denise grinned and then looked away.

"I know what you mean," agreed Carter. He thought the day was just about perfect. Glancing sideways, he sneaked a look at Denise. *She's not only pretty,* he thought, *she's smart and adventuresome, too.*

"Oh, Carter. Look!" Denise cried out, pointing at the deserted house. It was on fire! Flames danced across the roof and leapt into the sky. Smoke poured from the broken windows.

"My *bike!*" yelled Carter as he took off running. Denise followed. Reaching his cycle, Carter quickly pushed it away from the burning house. He motioned for Denise to get on. When she was settled, he put it in gear. They sped a safe distance away from the house before stopping.

They watched as the fire ate the old dried wood of the Robbins' house. In a matter of minutes, it was totally consumed in flames.

Carter glanced up at the white-hot sun. "It's plenty hot today---but not hot enough to make a house burst into flames," he muttered aloud.

"I think Daisy Robbins started the fire," said Denise. She was trying to think of a reason why the abandoned house had burst into flames.

Carter nodded. "Maybe. Or else something in the house created a fire.

Like a piece of glass reflecting the sun onto the wood."

"Maybe. Or maybe she just didn't want to leave any trace of her sad past behind. Now when people come out here, they won't be reminded of her murder," suggested Denise.

They stared at the burning house until their bodies couldn't take the heat any longer. Sweat poured from their skin, soaking their T-shirts and drenching their hair. Yet they were reluctant to leave. To them, the burning house was like a rite, a ceremony of beginnings and endings.

Finally, Carter put the bike in gear and they sped across the desert toward the highway. Before turning toward Palm Springs, Carter stopped. They took one last look back at the house. Now it was just a skeleton of flaming wood and black smoke.

The mystery is solved. And my visit is over, thought Denise. She wondered if her parents had patched up their marriage. She hoped so. Studying Carter's back, she smiled. She liked him—a lot. She would miss him.

After Carter drove into his parents' driveway, Denise dismounted. She walked with him as he pushed his bike into the garage. "I'll be going home tomorrow, Carter. I guess you'll be glad to get back to practicing for your motocross race."

Carter frowned. He already knew that he'd miss her. The last two weeks had been very special. "Yeah. I *do* need to practice. But I'm going to miss you." He grinned shyly at her.

"I'll sure miss you, too," Denise whispered. She leaned against him and planted a kiss on his cheek.

On the other side of the door leading into the house, Murphy began to bark and growl. They looked at each and laughed.